Aziza's Secret Fairy Door

and the Ice Cat Mystery

Lola Morayo

Illustrated by
Cory Reid

MACMILLAN CHILDREN'S BOOKS

With special thanks to Tọlá Okogwu

Published 2021 by Macmillan Children's Books
an imprint of Pan Macmillan
The Smithson, 6 Briset Street, London EC1M 5NR
EU representative: Macmillan Publishers Ireland Ltd, 1st Floor,
The Liffey Trust Centre, 117–126 Sheriff Street Upper
Dublin 1, D01 YC43
Associated companies throughout the world
www.panmacmillan.com

ISBN 978-1-5290-6395-0

Text copyright © Storymix Limited 2021
Illustrations copyright © Cory Reid 2021
Series created by Storymix Limited.
Edited by Jasmine Richards.

The right of Storymix Limited and Cory Reid to be identified as the
author and illustrator of this work has been asserted by them
in accordance with the Copyright, Designs and Patents Act 1988.

1 3 5 7 9 8 6 4 2

A CIP catalogue record for this book is available from the British Library.

Printed and bound by CPI Group (UK) Ltd, Croydon CR0 4YY

Chapter 1

'Pass the felt tip, please,' Otis asked, bending

over the piece of card in front of him.

Aziza stared at the jumble of coloured pens

littering the dining table. 'Err, which one?'

It was the first day of the holidays and she

and her brother were busy making Jamal Justice-themed Christmas cards to send to their family.

Otis's tongue was sticking out now in concentration. 'The dark red one, I need to get JJ's cape *just* right.'

Aziza rolled her eyes. Otis was obsessed with Jamal Justice, the superhero star of the graphic novels her parents wrote and illustrated.

'Here you go.' Aziza handed him the red pen. 'Can you pass me those sequins please?'

'You can't give JJ sequins.' Otis stared at her, horrified. 'Anyway, don't you think you've made everything sparkly enough?' He looked around the room.

Aziza followed his gaze. Twinkling fairy lights and glittery tinsel hung from *every* possible surface. She loved this time of the year and felt a fizz of excitement as she thought about all the fun things her family had planned.

Glittersticks, I missed a spot, Aziza thought, spying a tinsel-free corner by the speaker. *I'll add more later. Right now, I need to finish this card for Great Aunty Az.* But something wasn't

quite right. There was JJ in his superhero pose. He even had his Ray Atomizer. *So, what's missing?* Aziza nodded to herself. *I know. I'll add Peri and Tiko.* She missed her magical friends from Shimmerton.

Her hands flew over the sheet as she drew their bodies. One had a pair of feathery wings. The other a furry face.

'Why have you put a fairy and a bear on your card?' Otis peered at Aziza's drawing.

'He's not a bear, he's a—'

'Hey Zizzles, you still helping me with the cake later?' Dad asked, popping his head through the doorway.

Otis's face creased into a disgusted frown. He hated the Jamaican Christmas cake Dad insisted they make every year, but Aziza couldn't get enough of the sweet sticky stuff. She loved it almost as much as the spicy jollof rice Mum made during the holidays.

'Yes, please!' Aziza replied. 'I just need to finish this drawin—'

'Aziza's going on about fairies again,' Otis interrupted. 'She's even added a fairy and a bear to her card.'

'Good stuff. Zizzles has got an amazing imagination just like her Dad.'

'And her mother,' Mum called from the kitchen.

'That's right, honey,' Dad agreed. 'He turned back towards Aziza and winked. 'Let me know when you're done.' Then his head disappeared again.

It didn't take long for Aziza and Otis to finish making the cards AND tidy the table. Aziza spotted a box of left-over tinsel. It was crammed with different colours. She decided that she would deal with the tinsel-free areas in the flat and then go help her dad with the cake. While

Otis settled on the sofa to watch TV, Aziza set to work with the tinsel, whistling as she went.

Otis groaned. 'Cut it out, Zizi. I'm trying to watch the new episode of *Captain Bones*.'

'I'm not stopping you,' Aziza replied.

'You're whistling. *Really* loudly, and I can't see the screen past all that tinsel.'

Aziza gasped. 'But it's pretty.'

Otis rolled his eyes. 'Pretty awful you mean. And your whistling is terrible.'

'Well, that's not very nice—' she broke off as she noticed the teasing glint in Otis's eyes and realised he was just messing with her.

'I'm going to check if my room needs any more tinsel. Then I'm going to help Dad make your *favourite* cake,' Aziza announced. She started whistling again . . . even LOUDER and Otis's groan followed her as she left.

❀ ❀ ❀

'Hey Lil,' Aziza called to her peace lily as she entered her bedroom. 'You don't think my whistling is awful, do you?' She skipped past the fairy dolls and books lying on the floor and straight to the windowsill. 'Would you like some tinse—'

Aziza gasped. A thin white film of frost covered the plant's glossy green leaves, and they were beginning to droop. *Oh no. What's happened?* Aziza looked around in confusion. Her room wasn't cold, and the window was definitely closed.

'What's the matter, Lil?' Aziza whispered as she bent towards the little plant. She stopped as she spotted her fairy door that always stood next to Lil. It was covered in frost too.

The metal hinges and stick-on gem doorknob glinted white, like Mum's special cookies after she dusted them with icing sugar.

Is this the sign? Aziza wondered. Peri had told her before she left Shimmerton that the fairy door would let her know when it was time to return.

A tingle went through Aziza's fingers as she reached for the tiny doorknob. The fizzy feeling spread up her hand, then through her arm as a familiar warmth filled her whole body.

'It's happening again,' Aziza breathed.

Soon she was shrinking, and the glittering doorknob now filled her whole palm. It had transformed into a real jewel. She tugged on the door, but it wouldn't budge.

Aziza frowned. *This isn't right.* She tugged at the doorknob again, but still nothing. *It must be stiff from the frost*, she realised.

Aziza gritted her teeth and YANKED. The door swung open and a golden beam of light surrounded her. With a happy sigh, she stepped across the threshold and into the wonder beyond.

Chapter 2

Aziza was on the other side of the doorway, which faced out onto Shimmerton Green. Except it wasn't green anymore. Instead, the frost-tipped grass shone white in the afternoon sun.

I'm back! She gazed up at the familiar candyfloss-coloured sky with its spiral-shaped clouds. In the distance, she could see that a thick layer of frost covered Shimmerton's grassy hills and colourful houses. The frosty cobbled path which wound through the green was filled with Shimmerton residents who slipped and slid along it. Nearby, Aziza spotted a wooden bandstand filled with flowers. *Oh no*, she thought as she noticed the drooping heads of the blooms. *It must be too cold for them.*

But Aziza wasn't cold.

Her jumper and jeans were gone, replaced by the most gorgeous green velvet dress. The hem and sleeves were trimmed with lace and sewn-on sparkly silver stars. Even her pockets were edged with the pretty trim. She reached down to touch the delicate material and noticed that a piece of tinsel was poking out of her pocket.

Aziza smiled. *I bet Tiko will love it*. She pushed down the glittery tinsel so it was completely out of sight.

Aziza looked over her shoulder, checking on the secret fairy door. It was nestled into

the trunk of a big oak tree. She could hardly

tell it was there. *Good*, she thought. *I don't

want to risk anyone finding it.*

She grinned as she noticed that her

fairy wings were back as well. 'Yes!' Aziza whispered. The wings fluttered in anticipation, as if waving hello and saying, 'Let's go.'

Aziza shook her head. She wasn't going to start flying straight away. She'd save that for later when she met up with her friends Peri and Tiko. *Now, where are they?*

She stepped onto the wide cobbled path and instantly had to put her arms out to keep her balance.

'Imagine!' grumbled a deep voice from very nearby. 'Frost in Shimmerton in the middle of summer.'

It was Alf, the Elf and Safety Officer . . . and he didn't look too happy. Pushing a wheelbarrow full of salt, he shuffled along the path carefully. Every so often he'd stop and sprinkle salt onto the path, then mutter something under his breath.

Aziza gratefully stepped onto a gritted area and it was a lot less slippery. 'Thanks, Officer Alf,' she called but she wasn't sure if he heard her because of the very high pitched giggling that filled the air.

Aziza followed the sound and spotted three familiar fairies running along the path.

Oh no, it's the Gigglers! Aziza stepped behind a nearby tree. She really didn't fancy dealing with Kendra, Felly and Noon right now. Not unless Peri and Tiko were by her side. They were far too fond of tricks.

'Young ladies, please stop running on this

path,' Officer Alf said to the Gigglers. 'It's slippery and dangerous. Why don't you fly?'

'Sorry, Officer Alf,' they replied.

'It's not easy to fly when it's this chilly you know,' said Noon. 'Our wings get extra tired and cold.'

'Besides, we're practising our spells,' Felly said, waving something shiny in the air. 'Look! I've got a magic wand!'

Aziza shrank back against the tree. She thought fairies didn't get their wands until they were much older. The thought of a Giggler with actual magic was VERY scary.

Felly waved the wand. 'Noon is slow and has no fizz, make my magic the best there is!'

Nothing happened. There were no magical sparks or puffs of smoke. Aziza peered over at the 'wand'. *It's just an icicle,* Aziza realised with a sigh of relief. *They're just pretending.*

Noon tossed her head, her tight pink curls bouncing. 'I can do much better than that,' she said.

'Urgh, this is so totally boring,' Kendra said with a roll of her eyes. 'I don't want to play pretend magic. Let's go and find something else to do.' She stomped away and her friends chased after her.

Aziza sighed with relief and carried on

walking until she was at the centre of the Green.

'Aziza! You're back,' Tiko cried. He was carrying a huge stack of newspapers that almost completely hid his furry face.

'Told you she would be,' Peri said nudging Tiko. The pile of newspapers he was carrying wobbled dangerously. 'You owe me a wizzpop.'

'I missed you both.' Aziza said. 'I'd hug you but there are a lot of newspapers in the way. What are they for?'

'Officer Alf asked us to protect the flowers

on the bandstand from the frost. If we wrap them with these extra copies of the *Shimmerton Times*, that should warm them up.'

Aziza stared past the newspapers at Peri's top and shorts. 'You look like you could do with some layers to warm you up as well. What's going on with the weather? Officer Alf said it's the middle of summer.'

Peri shrugged. 'It's *supposed* to be summer but, all of a sudden, today it was freezing. No one knows why. My dad has the royal weathermen trying to work it out.'

'Luckily,' Tiko said. 'I'm always warm, but

in the winter I get the sneezey shapeshif—'
Tiko's little nose began to twitch. 'Oh furballs.
Not again. *ATISHOO!*'

Tiko's pile of newspapers went flying
everywhere, and by the time Aziza managed
to catch them, Tiko had transformed into the
most adorable baby goat.

'He was trying to say that he always gets a case of sneezy shapeshifting when it's cold. Everything is so confused.' She frowned. 'I mean look at him now . . . He's a Yule Goat!'

Aziza bent down and gave Tiko's head a quick scratch. 'What's a Yule Goat?' she asked him.

'Oh, you'll be lucky to get anything out of him when he's like that,' Peri said with a roll of her eyes. 'All he wants to do is chomp on stuff. A real Yule Goat would actually be out helping gnomes deliver presents.'

'But only at Christmas,' Tiko bleated. 'Lots

of creatures only come out then.'

'Like Santa's elves?' Aziza asked excitedly. 'I've always wanted to meet one.'

Peri shrugged. 'Nah, they're much too busy.' Her nose wrinkled. 'You're more likely to see the Yule Lads.'

'Who?' asked Aziza.

'The Yule Lads? They turn up in winter when it's cold,' Tiko said, stamping his hooves in excitement. 'We always leave out lots of treats, otherwise they play tricks on us. There are thirteen of them, but my mum thinks Pot Scraper is the best because he always licks

31

the pots clean and she doesn't have to do the dishes.'

Peri snorted. 'Well, let's hope they don't turn up. *My* dad says the Yule Lads are thoughtless pranksters. And if they come now when it's not even winter, no one will have any treats ready for them, so there's no telling what they'll do. It'll be chaos! Every year, Door Slammer keeps us up all night stomping around and slamming doors for fun. Do you know how many doors our palace has?'

'You have a point,' Tiko said.

Peri nodded. 'And last year they filled my

favourite trainers with rotting potatoes and didn't give me any treats, just because I was a little naughty.' She shivered. 'Come on, let's help wrap newspaper round those poor flowers. It's getting even colder.'

Aziza looked over at the flowers just in time to see Tiko hurtling towards them with a hungry expression.

'No, Tiko!' cried Aziza. She dropped the newspaper and dived forwards.

'*ATISHOO!*' sneezed Tiko, just as Aziza's arms clamped around him.

He blinked at her in surprise, back to his

normal self. 'Goodness, those flowers just

looked so yummy when I was a goat.'

The flowers hummed in reply, their petals vibrating a tune that sounded very disapproving, until Peri tucked some warm newspaper around them.

Just then, a unicorn wearing a tank top came galloping across the green. He shot past Aziza, Tiko and Peri, and speeded towards Officer Alf, who had finished gritting the path and was now on the grass.

'Steady on, Mr Bracken,' the Elf and Safety Officer cried to the unicorn. 'You'll do yourself an injury.'

'No time for that,' Mr Bracken

screeched to a sudden stop.

Officer Alf sniffed. 'There's always time for health and safety.'

'You don't understand.' Mr Bracken's breathing was heavy. 'Ccoa the Ice Cat

has been spotted in town, near the river. He doesn't look happy, and you know what that means. We must find him and return him to his home, or the whole of Shimmerton will freeze.'

Officer Alf swallowed hard. 'All right everyone!' he called loudly. 'Gather round, quickly now. We have a health and safety emergency and there's no time to lose!'

Chapter 3

Aziza and her friends joined Officer Alf.
He was trying to calm a stressed-looking
leprechaun whose beard was growing icicles.

'Patience, please.' Officer Alf sounded
flustered. 'As I said, Ccoa the Ice Cat

is in Shimmerton, and—'

'What?' interrupted an ogre with a ponytail. 'Shouldn't he be on Ice Mountain with that sorcerer of his?'

Officer Alf nodded. 'Clearly, something very odd has happened, and if he's upset that will cause more frost, and maybe even hailstorms.'

The leprechaun pulled an icicle from his beard. 'He must be VERY upset. This weather's awful.'

'Indeed,' agreed Mr Bracken, smoothing his tank top down. 'But what does Ccoa want in town?'

'Maybe he's lost?' suggested Tiko.

'Perhaps. Regardless, we must find the cat and coax him back up Ice Mountain before everything freezes over.' Officer Alf shuddered. 'We don't want the Yule Lads turning up early.'

A murmur of agreement ran across the small crowd.

'Why doesn't someone just go and speak to the sorcerer?' Peri asked. 'She must know where he is.'

Mr Bracken bowed low to Peri. 'Brilliant suggestion, Princess Peri, but we've already tried that. She's not at home either. The whole thing is a mystery.'

'OK! Here's the plan,' Officer Alf said.

'Fan out, work in teams. We need to find Ccoa. And quickly.'

Peri beamed at her two friends. 'Well, it's a good thing we've got the best team in town.'

Aziza gave Tiko a high five. 'You bet!'

Just then, Kendra rushed forward, pushing Aziza and Peri out of the way. 'Obviously, the Gigglers are here too, ready to help.'

Felly and Noon appeared at her side. 'We're all about helping the community.'

Peri rolled her eyes. 'Helping yourselves to other people's things maybe.'

Kendra whirled round. 'Who asked you?'

'Now, now, ladies,' said Officer Alf. He stepped between the two fairies. 'Kendra's offer is a generous one, and we'll need everyone's help to find Ccoa. Teamwork makes the dream work.'

Wouldn't it be better to find the sorcerer first, though? Aziza wondered, but she didn't feel confident enough to suggest it. She was still new to Shimmerton. *I'm sure everyone knows what they're doing.*

'I have an idea,' Kendra said looking at Aziza and her friends. 'Why don't we work together? After all, six pairs of eyes are better than three.'

Noon and Felly shared a confused look.

Peri frowned and crossed her arms. 'We're not working with you three. You can't be trusted.'

Mr Bracken gasped. 'That's not very nice, your Highness.'

Kendra gave a sad sigh. 'We *really* are only trying to be helpful.'

Aziza wasn't sure what to believe, but all the while the air was getting chillier. They didn't have time to argue.

Aziza lifted her chin. 'Fine, let's work together.'

Peri's jaw dropped. 'Huh?'

Kendra smirked. 'Thanks, new girl. When did you get back anyway?'

Aziza took a deep breath. 'That doesn't

matter. What's important is that if we work together, we'll find Ccoa faster. We need to stop this frost!'

'We should probably try the frostiest places first,' Tiko suggested as the whole gang left the green. 'Ccoa might still be down by the riv—'

'That's exactly what I was going to say,' Kendra interrupted. 'Let's try the playground. It's really frosty there.'

'How convenient,' Peri muttered.

The playground was empty when they arrived. The sea-horse see-saw had almost frozen solid and even the magical wings on the swings were shivering. But there was no sign of the Ice Cat. Next, Aziza, Tiko, Peri

and the Gigglers tried some of the winding paths that led off the main high street. They tried calling the cat's name.

Ccoa was nowhere to be seen.

'That cat's trickier than . . . Well, me,' Kendra complained.

'Maybe we should try tempting him with some milk?' Felly suggested.

Noon rolled her eyes. 'He's a magical Ice Cat that can control weather. He doesn't care about milk!'

'Why don't we try the river?' Tiko suggested. 'Didn't someone say he was spotted nearby?'

'Great idea, Tiko,' Aziza said. 'It's not too far.'

They arrived at the river and found

50

it was almost frozen solid.

'Wait! I see something.' Tiko pointed. 'It

looks like footprints.'

'What? Where?' Kendra demanded rushing forwards.

Noon and Felly chased after her.

'Hold up,' Aziza cried. 'Don't trample over the footprints . . .'

She trailed off as she looked down at the churned-up ground left behind by the Gigglers. It was too late.

'Look what you've done,' Peri cried. 'You've ruined the tracks.'

'They probably weren't Ccoa's anyway,' Kendra muttered.

'We'll never know now, will we?' Aziza

blew a breath of frustration.

'Look it's not our fau— Ow!' Kendra cried. 'Something just hit me on the nose.' She stared at Aziza, Tiko and Peri accusingly.

'Ow!' Tiko yelped. 'Me too.'

Peri looked up. Her eyes widened. 'Hail!' she yelled. 'Take cover.'

Tiko scanned the riverbank. 'No wait. I can see a Handy tree over there. It'll be safer.'

But the Gigglers weren't listening. They whizzed away, screeching, and flew to the nearest tree.

'Which way?' Aziza asked, dodging a huge

hailstone the size of a ping-pong ball.

'Follow me.' Tiko rolled himself into a ball and barrelled forwards.

Aziza wished she could do the same thing. She certainly wasn't going to try flying with all this hail about, but Peri was doing a great job of dodging the icy missiles.

'Aziza! Duck left,' Peri shouted from the air.

Aziza did. Just in time too, as another hailstone landed.

'Spin, Peri,' Aziza called out to her friend.

Peri did a perfect pirouette in the air,

narrowly missing a huge hailstone.

They arrived under the Handy tree, panting for breath and climbed up into the thick branches, which made a great perch. The leaves above them began to move, fusing together like a giant green hand and protecting them from the hail.

Wow! So that's why it's called a Handy tree, Aziza thought.

She grinned over at Tiko. 'I wish we had these trees at home.'

'They are pretty useful in a hailstorm,' Tiko said.

'Looks like the Gigglers agree.' Peri pointed ahead.

Heading straight for them were three very bedraggled fairies. Noon zigzagged wildly in the air dodging hailstones, knocking into Kendra who knocked into Felly.

Aziza frowned. 'Why aren't they working together?'

Peri just shrugged. 'They're Gigglers.'

Finally, the trio made it to the Handy tree.

'Told you we should have gone with them from the beginning,' Noon grumbled.

Felly nodded, and Kendra narrowed her eyes at her friends.

'We're all here now,' Aziza said. 'Let's just sit tight.'

Kendra wasn't listening. 'I'm starving. I'm going to collect some nuts.'

She flew up through the branches.

'Wait for us,' Felly and Noon chorused as they followed.

❀ ❀ ❀

In no time, they were back, and their pockets were bursting with nuts.

Aziza's stomach rumbled.

Felly offered her a nut. 'Want one?'

'Thanks.' Aziza took one, thinking that the Gigglers definitely weren't all bad. 'These look like chestnuts. Back home, we roast them at Christmas. We even have a song about it.'

'Ooh, I like songs!' Felly exclaimed. 'I have an amazing voice and Christmas songs are my favourite. I don't like it when they're too high, though. I'm not good with high notes.'

Felly launched into a song about magical cats, even as the hailstorm started to ease off. Her voice was so screechy poor Tiko had to cover his sensitive ears.

This WHOLE song must be too high! Aziza thought.

'See, I just can't hit that high note at the end,' Felly complained. 'That's the first thing I'm going to fix after Ccoa gives me some magic.'

Aziza looked at Peri in confusion.

Kendra glared at Felly, while Noon kept mouthing 'Be quiet'.

'I hope he likes nuts,' Felly continued, oblivious to it all. 'It's the best offering we've got, and Kendra says we'll only get Ccoa to give us magic if we give him a gift first.' Felly finally looked at Kendra and Noon. 'Isn't that right?'

Kendra rolled her eyes. 'You're such a blabbermouth.'

Aziza stared at Felly. 'Don't you care about saving Shimmerton?'

Felly waved a hand. 'That's more *your* thing.'

'Listen, an Ice Cat is seriously powerful and seriously rare,' Kendra explained. 'We just need help so we can find Ccoa before he disappears back up Ice Mountain. You don't care about magic, but we do, so why shouldn't we get some?'

'Kendra, this isn't about getting stuff,' Aziza explained. 'Ccoa is out there scared, and Shimmerton is freezing over.'

For a moment Kendra looked unsure.

'There's no point talking to them, Aziza,' Peri said. 'This team was never going to work!'

'We don't have to stay here and listen to this,' Felly said with a sniff.

'Yeah, it's well boring.' With a beat of her

shiny beetle wings, Kendra flew up into the air. 'We'll find Ccoa without your help *and* we'll get some magic as well. You'll see.'

Felly and Noon gave them a little wave and they zoomed away.

Chapter 4

'Right! We can't let the Gigglers get to Ccoa first,' Aziza declared. She shimmied down the Handy tree. The leaves above had parted to reveal a chilly but clear pink sky.

Tiko scrambled after her. 'How can we stop them?'

'They've got a head start now,' Peri added.

Aziza bit her lip. *Tiko and Peri are right*, she thought. *But maybe we need to be clever, not fast.*

'We don't need to catch up with them,' Aziza revealed. 'This is an Ice Cat mystery. We just need more clues to solve it.'

Tiko's eyes lit up in understanding. 'We could talk to people on the high street? Try to get more information?'

Aziza nodded.

The three friends hopped over the giant

hailstones that still littered the ground and raced back to Shimmerton High Street. Shoppers that weren't skidding and sliding on the icy cobbles were now tripping over the hailstones that covered the slippery ground.

It looks like a game of skittles, Aziza thought as a troll spun past her. *Ccoa's made such a mess.*

'Excuse me, have you seen a magical Ice Cat?' Peri asked, helping a tiny brownie up off the ground. 'Goes by the name Ccoa. Probably looks a bit upset?'

'I'm afraid not,' replied the brownie in a surprisingly deep voice. 'No one has been able to spot that cat.'

And so it went with each new person they asked. No one seemed to have seen him, or to have any clues where he might be.

'This isn't working,' Aziza sighed. 'By the time we find Ccoa, we will all be popsicles.'

Peri, shivering in her T-shirt, hugged herself. 'We need a new plan.'

Aziza hesitated.

'Well, I might have one, but . . .' her voice trailed off.

'What is it?' Tiko asked.

Aziza took deep breath. 'I think we've been looking at the mystery the wrong way round. We've been looking for Ccoa, but we should be trying to find the sorcerer instead.'

Peri's eyes lit up. 'Of course! She knows Ccoa better than anyone. She'll be able to find him easily.'

'That's a great plan,' Tiko said. 'Wish we'd thought of it earlier. We might have found Ccoa by now.'

Aziza's cheeks got warm despite the cold. She kicked a hailstone with her foot. 'Actually, I thought of it back on the green. When Officer Alf made his announcement.'

Peri nudged Aziza. 'You should have said something.'

'But I didn't like to, I'm still so new to

Shimmerton,' Aziza replied.

'So what?' Peri said. 'My dad says a good idea can come from anywhere so it's important to speak up. It's why his Shimmerton Council meetings take so long.'

'You're right, Peri,' Aziza said. 'Next time I will. But for now, let's ask around and see if anyone has seen the sorcerer.'

'Shall we start with the pharmacy?' Tiko asked, pointing to a shop with a bright green cross hanging above the door. 'It's still open.'

Peri wrinkled her nose. 'Why would the sorcerer need a pharmacy?'

'She must have come into town for something.' Tiko shrugged. 'Besides, a good idea can come from anywhere, right?' He grinned cheekily.

A little bell above the door tinkled as Aziza and her friends entered the shop. Rows of shelves lined the bright white walls, packed with coloured bottles and boxes. Strange

potions and lotions twinkled under the bright lights.

What's pickle pong rash cream? Aziza wondered reading one of the labels.

A bird-like creature with a long neck stood behind the counter, facing away from them. He turned, and the bright red feathers on his head crackled with flames. Pinned to his white lab coat was a badge that said Mr Phoenix.

'How can I help you today?' Mr Phoenix said, with a rustle of his fiery feathers. 'Perhaps an ambrosia tonic? A lot of people have coughs today. Or perhaps a dragon's breath lozenge for a sore throat?'

'Thank you but we don't need any medicine,' Aziza replied. 'We're actually trying to find someone. Would you be able to answer some questions please?'

Before Mr Phoenix could reply, a great big *BANG* shook the shop. Boxes and bottles tumbled to ground, their contents spilling everywhere.

What was that slam? Aziza wondered. *Did it come from the back of the shop?*

'Oh dear!' exclaimed Mr Phoenix. 'What's

going on back there?' He went to investigate.

Tiko looked around at all the mess. 'We might as well put all this stuff back. Who knows how long he'll be?'

Aziza picked up the nearest box and almost dropped it when it started to vibrate in her hand.

'Careful with those jumping jelly beans,' Peri warned. 'They're great for curing hiccups, but a nightmare to find if they get loose.'

'*Eurgh*,' cried Tiko, quickly pushing a bottle back onto the shelf. 'Tadpole Bubble Vitamins. Totally slimy and they wiggle all the way down.'

Just as Aziza was putting the last box back, Mr Phoenix shuffled back up to the counter.

'I couldn't spot anything. It's all very strange.' He scratched his head. 'Maybe it was the wind?'

Peri frowned, her face thoughtful.

'What were we talking about again?' asked Mr Phoenix.

'We're trying to solve a mystery,' Aziza explained. 'Have you seen a sorcerer recently? She lives in the mountains normally.'

Mr Phoenix's face lit up. 'You mean Anka? She came by yesterday. Don't see her nearly often enough.'

Tiko leant forwards. 'How come?'

'She only drops by once in a while,' Mr Phoenix replied. 'She picks up her very special lip balm. It's awfully cold in those mountains and chapped lips are no joke, indeed they're not.' Mr Phoenix peered at Aziza. 'Hang on a sec.' He picked out three small tubes of lip balm from the cabinet beside him. 'Here you go,' he said with a flourish. 'For helping me tidy up. You'll need it in this weather.'

'Thank you.' Aziza unscrewed the lid and took a sniff. 'It's

so sparkly and it smells like toffee.'

Peri and Tiko opened theirs eagerly.

'Mine tastes like strawberry trifle,' Peri said, smacking her lips happily.

Tiko grinned, his whole furry face glittery from using too much. 'You're both wrong. It's definitely chocolate sponge.'

'That blend is my bestselling lip balm,' Mr Phoenix explained. 'It's full of surprises. Anka loves the stuff.'

'I can see why,' Aziza said. 'Do you have any idea where she might have gone next?'

Mr Phoenix thought for a moment. 'I

remember she said something about needing a new snuggly cloak. She'd have gone to Neith the weaver for that, I reckon.'

'Our first proper clue,' Aziza cried. 'To the weaver's!'

Chapter 5

Peri's nose wrinkled. 'Oh my wings, what's that smell?' she demanded as they approached the weaver's shop.

The stench was even worse once they stepped through the door, and Aziza immediately saw why. The shop was a mess, with fabric and mannequins scattered everywhere. But the worst part were the piles of rotten potatoes spilling into every free space.

Hunched over a big pile of potatoes was a tall woman dressed in a red, woven dress. She was holding a dustbin bag. Her skin glowed emerald green and a crown sat wonkily on her head.

This must be Neith, Aziza thought.

'I said don't come ba—' Neith stopped suddenly when she spotted Aziza and her friends. 'Sorry, I thought you were one of those Yule Lads.'

'Yule Lads?' Aziza repeated. She remembered what Peri and Tiko had said about them earlier in the day. 'Are they in town?'

Neith glowered. 'Where do you think all these potatoes came from?' She chucked a particularly rotten spud into the dustbin bag. 'I had to change into a golden cobra just to get rid of them. One of the perks of being a part-time goddess.'

'Bet they didn't like that.' Peri chuckled.

Neith's green lips curved upwards. 'No, they didn't. They kept going on about shoes. Asking why I hadn't put one out.' She threw her hands up in the air. 'It's not winter, so why would I?'

'It's the frost,' Aziza explained. 'It's got everything topsy-turvy.'

'Well, I had no warning. And I've been quite good this year.' Neith bent down to gather up more mouldy potatoes. 'I deserve a present. Not all this.'

'We'll help you clean up,' Aziza offered.

The three friends set about helping Neith tidy up the shop. It was a big job, there were potatoes everywhere. *How did those get in here?* Aziza wondered as she emptied out an orange pair of gloves.

'This is going to be very bad,' Peri said, glancing out of the shop window. 'No one will have put their shoes out for the Yule Lads.'

Neith's expression turned fierce. 'Who knows what havoc those pesky brothers are wreaking all over Shimmerton.'

'I bet you it was Door Slammer back at the Pharmacy,' Peri added. 'I'd know that slam anywhere.'

Soon the shop was clean and Neith looked much happier. The three friends were just preparing to leave when Aziza spotted a snuggly-looking cloak hanging a hook. She slapped a hand to her forehead. *I can't believe we almost forgot.*

'Did a sorcerer called Anka buy a cloak recently?' Aziza asked.

'Why yes, she did,' Neith replied. 'She chose

a lovely grey woven cloak, with a fur trim.'

Tiko gave a yelp.

'Fake fur, of course,' Neith reassured him. 'It looked so good with her golden headdress.'

Tiko looked relieved. 'Did she say where she was going next?'

'To the pet care store to get something special for that cat of hers.' The goddess straightened her crown. 'She thinks the world of him.'

'Thanks for the information, Neith,' Aziza said.

'My pleasure, though I should be saying thank you for helping me clear up all those potatoes.' She pulled down three bundles from a shelf. 'Here take these. It's cold out there and I wove these myself.'

Neith handed each of them a red hat, with matching scarf and gloves.

'Wow. It's so soft,' Aziza whispered. She wrapped the scarf around her neck and it immediately turned pinky-purple. 'Thank you.'

'It's made of Egyptian mood linen,' Neith

said. 'It changes colour depending on your mood.'

The three of them said goodbye to Neith and stepped back out onto the cobbled street. 'The pet care store is this wa—' Tiko broke off as the sound of loud footsteps thundered towards them.

'Watch out,' Peri yelled. She pulled Tiko back, just as a little man with flushed red cheeks and a thick white beard dashed past. His arms were full of metal pots and his red hat flapped in the wind as he bolted down the high street. Right behind him was Mr Bracken, head down, with his horn pointed dangerously low.

'You come back here, Pot Scraper!' yelled the unicorn, as he dashed after the Yule Lad. 'Give me back my leftovers.'

Aziza looked around at Shimmerton's high

street. Tarts and doughnuts spilled out of the
bakery doorway mixed with yet more rotten
potatoes. Aziza could hear yelling coming
from inside. Hailstones still rolled along the

street and the frost was getting thicker.

A sudden loud scream filled the air.

'Come on,' Peri cried to the others. 'It's coming from the Teacup Cafe.'

They raced towards the scream and found two goblins trapped inside a teacup-shaped dining table that was totally out of control! Instead of slowly spinning on the spot it was whizzing round at an incredible speed.

Nearby, a creature – half human and half

horse – was wailing, 'Oh my poor customers.'

'That's Charlie the centaur, he owns the café,' Peri said. 'We should help.'

Just then, the teacup spun straight up into the air and there it hovered. The goblins screamed even louder.

'Oh dear,' Charlie moaned, as Aziza and her friends arrived at his side. 'Ice has got into the mechanism and the magic isn't working properly.'

'Those goblins must be getting so dizzy,' Peri said. 'We'll fly up and get them down. Right, Aziza?'

Aziza nodded eagerly, excited to use her wings again. *I just need a happy thought.* That's how she flew last time she was in Shimmerton. Aziza imagined her family back home and let the warmth of the thought flow through her body until she tingled. Then with a wiggle of her shoulders, she shot up through the air. Peri flew close behind her. *This feels amazing!*

The goblins' screaming was even louder now Aziza was in the air and closer to them. 'It's OK. We're here to help!' she shouted, but the goblins were too busy wailing to hear her.

'It's no use,' Peri said. 'They're too scared to listen.'

'We need to calm them down. I think I have an idea to distract them.' Aziza turned back to the goblins. 'You know, when it starts to get chilly like it is right now, I know Christmas is on its way. I get to make cards and decorate with tinsel. What about you, Peri?'

Peri's tapped her lip thoughtfully. 'It's all about the food for me when I want to celebrate. Sticky baklava with pistachios is my favourite.'

At the mention of food, the goblins stopped screaming.

'I like celebrating with food,' said one.

The other goblin rubbed his pointy chin. 'Nectar cups are the best thing to celebrate midsummer's eve.'

It's working! Aziza thought. *The goblins are much calmer.* But Aziza didn't know how she was going to get them down and her wings were almost completely numb with cold. *I don't think I can stay up here much longer.*

A loud sneeze came from the ground below, then a shadow appeared, and Aziza turned to find a ginormous yeti behind her. His shaggy white fur sparkled, and his dark nose was . . . twitching?

'Tiko!' Aziza cried.

He reached out and scooped up the startled goblins, before setting them gently back on the ground. Aziza and Peri followed swiftly.

'You sneezy shape-shifted again, didn't you?' Peri said with a grin.

Tiko grinned back. 'I'm just glad it wasn't a Yule Goat again.'

'Oh, thank you so much, you three.' Charlie the centaur was beaming. 'I've got

something for you.' He disappeared inside, returning a few moments later with three steaming mugs of hot chocolate.

'This is delicious.' Peri licked some chocolate off her top lip.

'And just the right temperature too.' Warmth spread through Aziza's body, right from her toes to the very tips of her wings. 'I feel amazing!'

'It's a secret Centaur family recipe.' Charlie said with a wink. 'And maybe even a little bit magical. Enjoy! You three deserve it.'

Chapter 6

The pet care store looked dark and gloomy
from the outside. 'Are you sure we'll find a
clue in there?' Tiko did not sound convinced.

'Neith said this is where Anka the sorcerer
went next,' Aziza reminded him.

'I hope she's right . . .' Peri's voice trailed off as they entered the shop.

It was like stepping into a jungle. The air was warm and humid. Broad green leaves and long tangled vines hung from the ceiling. From somewhere deep in the shop came a low growl, followed by an answering hoot. The noise seemed to spark something because suddenly the shop was buzzing with the sounds of every animal and creature you could imagine. It was like being at the zoo at lunch time.

'I thought they only sold pet care products,'

Aziza yelled over the noise. 'Not the actual

pets.'

'They do. That's what's making all that

racket.' Peri picked up a dog collar. 'See?'

'Woof!' went the collar and

Aziza jumped back.

Woah! A barking

dog collar.

'This one is my

favourite,' said Tiko

and he picked up a hummingbird feeder.

Immediately it started chirping and hooting.

'It's always really noisy in here.'

'They're trying to get our attention,' Peri explained. 'They want us to buy them.'

Aziza peered at the shelves in fascination. A chew toy stared back at her, then smiled a wide Cheshire Cat grin. In another corner, a small dog basket was snoring.

'I wonder where Bissi is?' Tiko asked. 'She's the sprite who owns this shop,' he added.

The three friends continued through the shop till they came to a big fridge with glass doors. It was packed with bottles of milk. A creature about the height of a tin of baked beans was just shutting it.

Aziza stared, impressed. *She's much stronger than she looks.*

The creature twirled in mid-air, looking flustered.

'Hi, Bissi,' Peri said.

'Apologies, your highness,' Bissi replied with a curtsey. 'I've just been dealing with a Yule Lad problem.'

'They've been here too?' Peri asked.

Bissi snorted in annoyance and pointed to the fridge. 'I had to chuck one of them out after he tried to get into the full-moon milk.'

Aziza gaped. She couldn't imagine such a

tiny creature taking on a whole Yule Lad.

Bissi continued. 'I shudder to think what would have happened if he'd managed to steal some. There'd be some very grumpy cats in Shimmerton, that's for sure.'

'Wait. Did you say cats?' Aziza asked.

 'Oh yes,' Bissi replied, an amused smile curving her lips. 'I've yet to meet a cat who didn't love a saucer of full-

moon milk. It's why cat owners come from miles away just to get some,' she added proudly.

Glittersticks! Aziza clapped her hands. *That must be why Anka came here.*

'Has a sorcerer from Ice Mountain bought some by any chance?' she asked Bissi.

Bissi nodded. 'How did you know? She dropped by yesterday, said it was her last stop of the day.'

'Did she say where she was going next, by any chance?' Peri asked.

'Straight home to Ice Mountain if I

remember correctly. She was missing that cat of hers.' Bissi fluttered past them. 'Now if you'll excuse me, I better go check if any of my dog collars need feeding.'

'OK, so we already know that Anka wasn't at her house,' Peri said as they left the pet care shop. 'Mr Bracken checked.'

'So, where could she be?' asked Tiko.

Aziza thought for a moment, then an icy sign ahead caught her attention.

'I know!' Aziza pointed to the sign. 'We'll retrace her route home. She didn't get to her house but what if that's because she stopped somewhere else on the way?'

'It's worth a go,' Peri said. 'If we find her, I just *know* she'll be able to help us with Ccoa.'

'Poor cat,' Tiko sighed. 'He must be scared. No wonder he's so upset.'

Aziza and her friends raced past the sign, then followed it onto a frosty path that wound away from town and towards the mountains. At last, they came to edge of a thick and dark forest. The trees stretched high into the sky, their gnarled branches a twisty warning.

Aziza swallowed. 'This place looks proper scary.' A low wail echoed through the tress. 'It even *sounds* creepy.'

'It's called the Wailing Woods for a reason,' Peri replied.

This way to Ice Mountain

'We've not visited for ages,' Tiko said. 'Not since the duende moved in.'

'What's a Dwenday? And what's so scary about it?' Aziza asked.

Peri grimaced. 'It's pronounced *Doo-en-day* and it likes to lure people into the woods, so they lose their sense of direction and get hopelessly lost.'

Tiko shivered. 'My mum says you do NOT want to meet one. They'll trick you and make you disappear with their magical whistling.'

As if in answer a strange whispering sound

came from somewhere behind them.

'What's that?' Peri squeaked.

The trio turned quickly, but there was no one there. Just a huge boulder.

'It's the wind.' Aziza's voice was a little shaky. 'Right?'

Tiko's nose twitched furiously. 'I don't like this at all.'

They turned back towards the woods. No one wanted to go inside now. *But we have to,* Aziza realised. *We have to, if we're going to solve this mystery.*

Aziza straightened. 'We can do this.

Anka might need our help.'

A twig snapped behind them. The three friends shared a terrified look and then they slowly turned around.

Chapter 7

'Surprise!' Kendra cried, jumping out from behind the boulder.

There was a high-pitched giggle, then Felly appeared. 'Did you see their faces?'

'Almost as funny-looking as yours,' Noon

replied striding into the clearing.

Felly's laughter stopped abruptly. 'That's well rude.'

Aziza shook her head. 'What are you guys doing here?'

Kendra smirked back. 'We've been following you, obviously.'

So that's the whispering noise we heard earlier, Aziza realised. *Not the wind!*

Peri's eyes narrowed. 'You still think we'll solve the mystery for you and find Ccoa?'

'Pretty much,' Kendra said. 'So, hurry up and find the sorcerer and her cat so we

118

can get some magic powers.'

Peri stamped her foot in annoyance. 'You can't just get us to do all the hard work for you!'

'Yes, actually. We can,' Felly said.

'Besides, we don't like it in town right now,' Noon said. 'There are far too many Yule Lads about and they keep on telling us that we've been naughty.'

Aziza raised an eyebrow but didn't say anything.

Kendra crossed her arms. 'Are we going into these woods or what?'

Tiko's nose was twitching furiously. 'You don't understand, there's a duende in there!'

Kendra huffed. 'I'm not afraid of the forest or any silly old duende.' She waved a hand airily. 'Besides, you can't believe everything you hear. Sometimes you've got to make up your own mind about what scares you.' She took

120

a determined step towards the path. 'You lot coming or what?' she called over her shoulder.

Peri raced to get in front of Kendra. 'You're not in charge.' The girls squabbled all the way into the thick forest as they led them all deeper into the gloom.

The tall trees loomed over the group like gnarled and twisted giants. Hazy pink light streamed through their thick trunks, breaking into a kaleidoscope of colours. Everything was quiet, but every so often, a high-pitched wail would echo through the trees.

'Something's coming,' Felly cried, moving

closer to Noon. 'I can hear it.'

'Where?' Noon screeched, spinning in a circle. 'I can't see anything.'

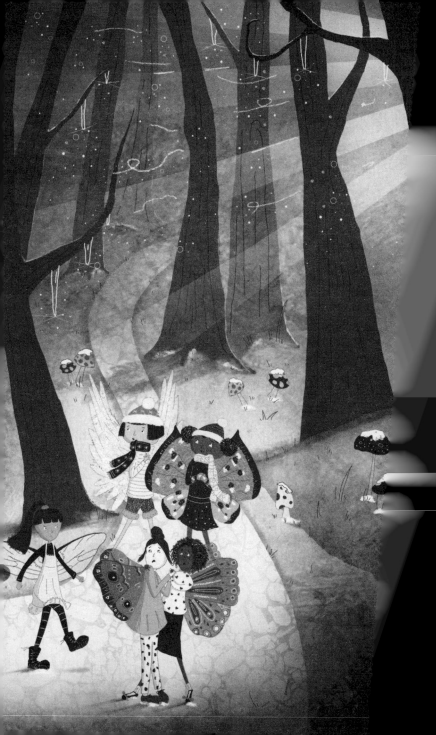

'Oh, calm down, you two,' Kendra snapped. 'It's just the wind blowing through the leaves and branches.' She pointed at a dense line of trees. 'See?'

Felly squinted at them. 'Oh . . . so that's why it's called the Wailing Woods.'

Kendra rolled her eyes and continued walking.

'It's actually quite soothing,' Noon said. 'Bit like the wind chimes at the top of Giggleswick Street.'

Felly nodded eagerly. 'I guess the woods aren't as scary as I thought they would be.'

124

Probably because we're all together, Aziza thought. *I'm not sure I'd like to come here on my own.*

Peri leant towards Aziza. 'I do wish they'd be quiet,' she whispered.

Aziza smiled, but she secretly liked the Gigglers' non-stop chat. *If there was anything scary in these words, all the chatter would scare them off!*

Suddenly, an orange glow cut through the pink sheen of light that blanketed the forest. With it came the warm smell of spices.

Aziza sniffed. 'Can everyone smell that?'

'I can.' Tiko's little nose was twitching. 'It smells like cinnamon.'

'And nutmeg,' Felly added.

Peri was frowning. 'Why can we smell spices in the woods? I bet it's one of the duende's tricks.'

Kendra sniggered. 'Are you seriously scared of a mixed spice blend?' She strode ahead.

Once again, the others followed. The path widened and the trees opened up to reveal large cave set inside of smooth rock face. The same orange glow blazed from its entrance.

'It looks so warm in there,' Aziza breathed. 'And the air smells so nice.' She sniffed again. 'It's honey and even chocolate.'

'I'm really hungry,' Noon said with a longing sigh.

Tiko's nose began to twitch. 'I don't know about this. What if Peri is right and this is some kind of trap?'

'There's six of us,' Kendra scoffed. 'I'm going in to see what's what. You can stay here if you want.' She marched straight into the cave.

127

'We can't let her go by herself,' Aziza said, chasing after her. The others followed and the cave soon opened out and they found themselves in a large room lit by candles.

That mouth-watering aroma drifted across

the room and Aziza realised it was coming

from the candles. The hard rock floor was

covered by a thick plush rug, and wooden

shelves crammed with little trinkets lined the

smooth rock walls. Thick green garlands with

red berries hung across the wooden furniture and fireflies nestled in them like twinkly little fairy lights. A fire roared in a corner of what looked like a kitchen and in the centre of the room sat a wooden table.

It was occupied.

A small elf-like creature with oversized pointy ears and an equally big nose sat opposite a woman with bronze skin. Her face was partly hidden by a beautiful gold headdress studded with colourful gemstones. They were laughing and playing . . . chess? *Could this be Anka*, Aziza wondered.

But who's that with her?

'Dear me, we have company,' the small elf cried, spotting his visitors for the first time. He jumped up from his chair and bustled over to them. 'My name is Duende. Welcome to my home. Can I get you a drink, or maybe something to eat?'

Aziza blinked. *Duende? He's not at all scary.* She stepped forward. 'Thank you, but we actually need to speak to Anka urgently.'

The sorceress hadn't moved since they arrived but at the sound of her name, her head lifted slowly. Bright hazel eyes blinked back at Aziza from beneath the golden headdress.

'Me?' Anka said in a soft voice. 'Whatever for?'

'It's Ccoa,' Aziza replied. 'While you've been away, he's been wandering about Shimmerton causing hailstorms and frost. Even the Yule Lads turned up early.'

'Oh dear. Have I been gone that long?' Anka stood up from the table, revealing a brightly coloured robe. 'I feel awful. I got caught in a terrible summer storm yesterday. Then I heard someone whistling a happy tune and followed it here.' She smiled at the little elf. 'Dear Duende has been such a welcoming host, I must have lost all track of time.'

Duende wrung his hands. 'I feel terrible too because this keeps happening. It's just so important to me that people feel welcome when they visit, but then they never want to leave again.' He sighed. 'It's given me a dreadful reputation.'

'We know.' Kendra smirked. Everyone in Shimmerton thinks

you make people disappear.'

Duende's face fell.

'It must just be one big misunderstanding,' Aziza said quickly. 'You seem very nice, and I can see why people would want to stay.'

'Please,' Duende pleaded. 'You must let me make amends. I'm sure I can use my whistling to bring Ccoa back.'

'How does whistling help?' Aziza asked confused.

'If I think of someone and whistle, my magic calls them to me at extraordinary speed.' Duende looked at Anka. 'I just need a description of Ccoa.'

Anka tilted her head. 'He has the most gorgeous grey coat with black stripes that shimmer in the snow.' Then a slow smile spread across her face. 'His head is rather on the big side, and he's *very* sensitive about it.'

Duende blinked. 'Erm, anything else?'

'Oh yes, he has a habit of spraying hailstones from his eyes and ears. It's terribly cute.'

Everyone stared at Anka in shock. Aziza was no longer sure if they *should* bring Ccoa back. *He sounds awfully scary.*

Duende looked about his cosy house doubtfully. 'Perhaps we'd better step outside for this.'

Once everyone was outside the cave, Duende pursed his lips and whistled loudly three times, then paused and waited.

All was still and silent in the forest.

Duende looked perplexed. 'That *is* strange.'

'What?' cried Anka.

'My whistling didn't work.' Duende frowned. 'And that's *never* happened before.'

Chapter 8

'Wow! Awkward,' Kendra said. She turned to Anka. 'Can't you use your magic to bring Ccoa here?'

Anka shook her head. 'My magic comes from Ccoa. No cat. No magic.' She wrung her hands. 'I wonder why he didn't come.'

Maybe he's scared, Aziza thought. When she was scared in the forest it was the fact that there were six of them that made the difference.

'I think we should all whistle,' Aziza said. 'We'll be much louder if we do it together and Ccoa will be able to hear us.'

Duende looked thoughtful. 'It would certainly amplify my magic.' Then he nodded once. 'Yes, I think it would work if you all joined in.'

So they whistled. Together. It was not at all

in tune, but it didn't seem to matter because after a few seconds, they heard something scampering up the path.

Then a huge cat-like creature burst out of

the undergrowth. His black stripes shimmered against grey fur and glowing eyes glinted almost as brightly as the hail falling from them. *Wow!* Aziza thought. *He's not scary, he's beautiful.*

But Ccoa did not seem happy at all.

'Hello, my sweet,' Anka called to him, but he just growled angrily, refusing to look at her.

'Do you have a saucer?' The sorcerer asked Duende.

Duende bustled back into the cave, returning quickly with a small blue saucer.

Anka reached into a hidden pocket in her robe and pulled out a familiar bottle. It was the full-moon milk from the pet care store!

She filled the saucer and offered it to Ccoa in a soothing voice. The big cat sniffed the air once, then recognising the scent, he began to drink. Once he'd finished, he pushed the saucer away then promptly turned his back.

His tail lashing from side to side.

'Oh dear. He really is unhappy with me,' Anka said. 'I don't blame him. He must have been so very worried about me.'

'Maybe he'd like some nuts?' Kendra leapt forwards. 'I bet it'll even make him happy enough to give us magical powers.' She laid the nuts the Gigglers had gathered on the ground. Ccoa didn't even turn, but the growl he made sent Kendra scuttling backwards.

Anka chuckled. 'Nice try, but Ccoa can't grant magical powers to anyone other than me. We are completely tied to each other.'

Kendra scowled.

'I really wish we were home,' Anka said anxiously. 'I don't have any more milk or food, or anything shiny. Ccoa loves shiny things.'

Aziza's shoulders dropped in disappointment. *If we don't make him happy soon, the frost will never leave.* Aziza shoved her hands in her pockets in frustration. Something tickled her fingers. *TINSEL!*

Aziza quickly pulled the gold and silver tinsel from her pocket. Creeping forwards, she dangled it in front of the cat. His oversized

head turned slowly as he spied the shiny decoration. A big paw reached out, smacking at it playfully, then the other paw joined in. Finally, the magical cat nodded and let out a satisfied purr.

'Oh, you did it! Thank you so much,' Anka cried.

Peri grinned at Aziza. 'Mystery solved, sorcerer found and cat happy.'

Aziza nodded. *I wish Otis could see this,* she thought. *My whistling and tinsel helped to bring back Ccoa and save Shimmerton from an early winter!*

Everyone was happy. Except for Duende.

'What's the matter?' Aziza asked the little elf.

Duende shrugged. 'Oh, don't mind me. It's just been so nice to have you all. I so rarely get company.'

'Why don't you come back to town with us?' Peri suggested. 'The river is frozen, and we could all go ice skating before it melts.'

Duende shifted uneasily. 'Oh, I really couldn't. My reputation you see.'

Aziza took his hand reassuringly. 'Don't

worry,' she said patting it gently. 'We'll tell everyone how helpful you've been and that we wouldn't have found Ccoa without you.'

Anka coughed once and all eyes turned to her. 'Actually, I think I can do even better than that.' She closed her eyes and muttered some strange words under breath. The air fizzed with energy.

'What did you do?' Felly asked with a wide-eyed stare.

Anka smiled. 'You'll just have to trust me.'

❀ ❀ ❀

The journey back to Shimmerton town centre was swift. Ccoa scampered about, weaving happily between his new friends. Everywhere his feet touched, the frost magically melted away. *It's like it was never there*, Aziza thought, full of wonder.

As soon as they arrived in town, a very excited Elf and Safety Officer came dashing towards them, waving a newspaper.

'Have you seen this?' Officer Alf cried, shoving the paper into Aziza's hands. It was the *Shimmerton Times*.

THE SHIMMERTON TIMES

Wonderful Duende Whistler saves the day in Wailing Woods.

Inside were even more details about Aziza, Tiko and Peri and their successful investigation to find Anka. It even mentioned the Gigglers, though Kendra wasn't too impressed that her name wasn't in the headline.

Anka had a knowing, pleased look on her face. *That's what she was doing, Aziza*

150

thought. *She must have cast a spell to make this happen.*

Officer Alf took Duende's hand and shook it rapidly. 'On behalf of Shimmerton, I'd like to thank you for getting our beloved town out of the deep freeze.'

Duende sniffed, wiping away a tear with his free hand. 'This truly is the best gift ever. I feel like celebrating!'

'Yes, let's!' Peri cried.

And so they did. After melting all the remaining frost, Ccoa left the river till the very last so everyone could go skating . . .

Even the Yule Lads joined in.

'Wheee!' squealed Door Slammer, as he

whizzed past Aziza, Tiko and Peri. He gave

them a little wave and the three smiled back

nervously.

'Do you think Anka put a spell on them

as well?' Aziza said. 'They're being really nice.'

Tiko grinned, then pointed. 'If she did, she must have cast one on the Gigglers too.'

Aziza followed his direction and sure enough, the Gigglers were heading straight towards them. The three fairies spun and twirled happily around Aziza and her friends, until everyone was dizzy with laughter.

I guess they're not so annoying after all, Aziza thought as she watched them zoom away again.

'I was wrong, you know,' Peri said.

154

'Working with the Gigglers turned out to be a good thing.'

Aziza nodded. 'Without Kendra leading the way, we'd never have made it through the woods.'

❀ ❀ ❀

Soon the sun began to fade, and dusk fell across Shimmerton. *It's getting late*, Aziza realised. *I'd better get home. I still have to finish decorating my room and make the cake with Dad.*

The Yule Lads must have had the same thought, as they set off with a wave and a promise to be back when the real winter came.

'You'd better have those shoes ready,' Pot Scraper called over his shoulder, as his twelve brothers hurried away.

'We should be going too,' Anka said, giving her huge cat at pat on the head. 'Ccoa needs his beauty sleep.'

'May I escort you back through the woods?' Duende asked.

Anka giggled. 'That would be splendid.'

With hugs and kisses, Aziza said goodbye to her new friends before they set off back towards Ice Mountain.

'Can't you stay a bit longer?' Tiko asked

156

Aziza with a sad frown.

Aziza shook her head, not trusting her voice. 'Time passes differently at home, but I have to go back eventually.'

Peri sniffed. 'Come on, we'll walk you to the fairy door.'

The green looked completely different now all the frost had melted. The big oak tree sat exactly where she'd left it and Aziza breathed a huge sigh of relief when she spotted the fairy door still nestled safely within its trunk. Aziza drew close and the door began to shimmer. It was as if it sensed that her time in Shimmerton was up.

Tiko wrapped his arms around Aziza. 'You'll come back again soon?'

'Try and stop me,' Aziza said, squeezing him tight.

'Just keep an eye on the door,' Peri

reminded Aziza as she gave her a hug. 'It'll

let you know when it's time.'

Aziza nodded and with one last look at her

friends, she turned the jewelled handle and stepped through the door. With a flash of light, Aziza found herself back in her room. She stared at the fairy door, which was once again its usual size. She couldn't help the big grin that spread across her face. *What an amazing adventure!*

Tired from all the ice skating, Aziza laid down on her bed. Her eyes widened as they caught sight of the ceiling and she sat bolt upright again. Someone had written *We Woz Here* across her ceiling using fairy lights.

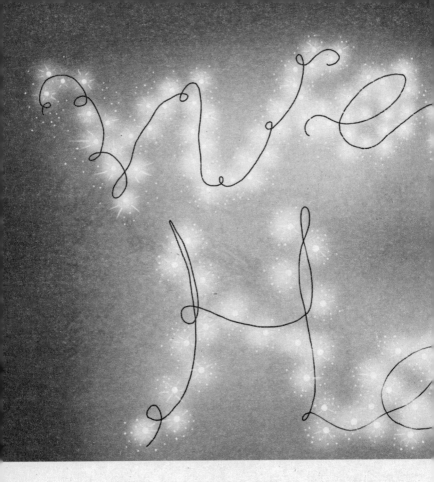

Aziza blinked in shock, unable to believe

what she was seeing. Could it have been

those cheeky Gigglers sneaking through the

fairy door? *I'll have to ask them next time I go to*

Shimmerton, Aziza thought. *And I'll be sure to*

take a dictionary too.

Myths and Legends

Aziza, her friends, and the inhabitants of Shimmerton are inspired by myths and legends from all around the world:

Aziza is named after a type of fairy creature. In West African folklore, specifically *Dahomey mythology*, the Aziza are helpful fairies who live in the forest and are full of wisdom.

Peri's name comes from ancient Persian mythology. Peris are winged spirits who can be kind and helpful, but they also sometimes enjoy playing tricks on people. In paintings they are usually shown with large, bird-like wings.

Ccoa comes from Peruvian folklore. The ccoa is a cat-like creature and the companion of a mountain god. It can bring about storms, hail and lightning.

There are many famous **centaurs** in Greek mythology. Like Charlie, they are all half human and half horse.

Duende (pronounced Doo-en-day) is a small, elf-like creature that gets its name from the Spanish word for goblin. Duendes appear in the myths of many other cultures too. Some are helpful. Some are sneaky. Some have magical powers.

Neith is the ancient Egyptian goddess of war and weaving. The Egyptians believed she was wise, powerful and helped settle disputes between other gods.

Phoenixes, like Mr Phoenix, are mystical,

bird-like creatures found in Greek mythology. They are said to be immortal and have healing powers.

Unicorns have appeared in folklore for thousands of years. Like Mr Bracken, they're normally portrayed as magical, horned white horses and are said to have healing powers.

Yule lads are the thirteen merry but mischievous Father Christmases found in Icelandic folklore. Each has a distinct personality. They visit children in the thirteen nights leading up to Christmas.

Join Aziza on her brand new
magical adventure in

Coming in February 2022

Chapter 1

'I'm running out of time,' Aziza sighed as she stared down at the piles of multicoloured paper and the half-completed invitations to her brother Otis's surprise birthday party. The party she was organising . . . well, trying to anyway.

Aziza picked up an invitation and stared at the picture of Jamal Justice on the front. Otis loved the superhero star of their parents' graphic novels. He was the perfect theme for the party, but there just didn't seem to be enough time to get everything done. The party was only a week away.

Aziza blew out a frustrated breath. *It's got to be special, but I don't know what to do first.*

'Hey, Zizzles,' a voice called out and Aziza quickly stuffed the invitations out of sight. But it was just her parents. Otis was nowhere to be seen.

2

'How are you getting on with the party planning?' her dad asked, coming into the living room.

'I'm not,' Aziza muttered. 'I still haven't finished the invitations.' She waved towards the pile on the floor. 'I still need to work out what music to play,' she continued, her voice getting squeaky.

Mum winced, knelt down and placed a finger under Aziza's chin, tilting her face up.

'I know it was your idea to give Otis a surprise party but we are here to help, you know. You don't have to do this by yourself.'

'I used to be a DJ. I could help pick the songs?' Dad offered with a grin.

'I need songs from this century, Dad,' Aziza replied. She shook her head. 'I can do it. I *want* to do it.'

'Okay, Zizzles,' Dad said. 'Just remember, the smartest people ask for help.'

Mum gave Aziza's nose an affectionate tap before she and Dad left the room.

Aziza stared after them. *Maybe I could get them to help with the cutting? Or the gluing? Or writing out the—*

Otis whizzed into the room at full speed.

'Yo, Zizi. Want to play fairy pirates?'

Aziza shook her head and started packing up the party stuff so Otis wouldn't see.

'I can't, I'm too busy.' Aziza's voice wobbled. Seeing him just made her even *more* worried that she was going to mess his party up.

Her brother peered at her. 'What's wrong with you? You look just like you did when I buried your fairy doll in the sandpit . . . Then forgot where I put her.'

Otis's words were the final straw, especially as she couldn't actually tell him anything without ruining his birthday surprise.

'Just leave me alone.' Aziza leapt up from the carpet. She dashed past a startled Otis and headed straight for her bedroom. She shut the door, grabbed her Fairy Power cushion from her bed and gave it a hug. Somehow the soft plush made her feel a bit better.

There was a rattling sound from the windowsill. Aziza's gaze went to the wooden fairy door that stood there – it was sparkling.

Aziza gasped as a cute ribbon magically unfurled around the edges of the door and tied itself in a messy bow. It could only mean one thing. *I'm going back to the magical kingdom of Shimmerton!*

Tingling with excitement, Aziza moved towards the fairy door. She untied the bow. The ribbon was smooth and soft beneath her fingertips. Next, she gently took hold of the bejewelled doorknob and felt a glowing warmth fill her whole body as the fairy door swung open. Then she was shrinking, and a golden beam of light surrounded her.

Aziza stepped through and into a magnificent ballroom. Once it had closed, the fairy door was hardly noticeable in the wall behind her. All around, creatures were dressed in beautiful party clothes and chattered and giggled. Huge balloons swooped and twirled in the air, lit up by twinkling fairy lights. Bright tapestries covered the walls, illuminated by big glowing lanterns.

'Where am I?' Aziza whispered. She looked down at herself, curious to see what she would be wearing this time. She gasped at the sight of the beautiful party dress, covered in shining silver stars that sparkled under all the lights. Her butterfly wings were back too, and Aziza gave them a little flutter.

I'm at a party! Aziza thought with a grin.

Just then, a small bear-like creature in a waistcoat bustled past. He had a clipboard in his hand and a worried frown on his face.

'Tiko!' Aziza called out, happy to see her little shape-shifting friend. She hadn't recognised him at first with his smart waistcoat on. Tiko looked up, his frown melting away when he spotted Aziza.

'Oh, goodness, I'm so pleased to see you,' he said.

'What's going on?' Aziza asked. 'Where are we?'

'It's Peri's birthday party, and I'm the official palace party planner,' Tiko replied. 'Peri wanted to organise the party without her parents' help, but I'm allowed to assist.'

Aziza grinned at him. How funny it was that her friends had been organising a party while she'd been doing the same thing at home for Otis. 'I bet you're doing an amazing job.'

'I hope so.' Tiko waved the clipboard about. 'We promised the king and queen we'd throw the best royal party ever!'

'Well, everyone looks like they're having a great time,' Aziza said, looking at the party guests. 'Besides, I'm here now and I can help.'

Tiko nodded. 'I'm *so* glad you are here. We weren't sure how to invite you.' Then he grinned. 'It's a good thing that fairy door always knows what to do.'

Aziza hugged that thought to herself. The door really did know and, with the way time froze at home while she was in Shimmerton, she didn't have to hurry back either. Besides, helping with Peri's party might give her some ideas.

'Would you like a drink?' Tiko asked as he led Aziza to a long banquet table, filled with the yummiest looking food and the most colourful drinks.

'Wow, this looks amazing.' Aziza picked up a sparkling pink glass and took a sip. 'It tastes like strawberries and sherbet fizzing inside my mouth.' She giggled. 'It's tickly.'

Tiko looked pleased. 'We have something for everyone. Buttercup slushies for the unicorns. Lime and honeysuckle smoothies for the pixies. There's even chocolate and carrot-flavoured milkshake for Mrs Sayeed's son.'

Tiko pointed to a happy-looking young almiraj, who wore a party hat. His bunny ears stood up in delight each time he took

12

a sip of the delicious milkshake.

Everyone looked as if they were having fun.

Aziza spotted an older fairy with a neat moustache, wearing a crown. He had wings of swan-like feathers. Beside him was a fairy in silk robes with long, flowing dark hair and a glittering headpiece. They were busy greeting guests. *They must be the king and queen,* Aziza thought. *Peri's parents. But where is their daughter?*

'Where's Peri?' Aziza asked Tiko.

'Up in her room, but she should really be down here by now.' Tiko looked up at a big golden clock on the wall. 'Don't suppose you could get her? She'll be so excited to see you.'

Without waiting for a reply, he reeled off a series of directions. 'Oh, and tell her not to forget the presents,' Tiko added before bustling away.

Forget the presents? Aziza was confused. Surely Peri wouldn't have been given her presents yet? She shrugged and set off to find her friend.

Outside the ballroom, Aziza walked along the hallway decorated with golden, scalloped tiles and jewelled borders, just like Tiko had described. She'd never seen anything so beautiful, until she turned right and caught a glimpse of the staircase. It was golden too!

'Glittersticks!' Aziza whispered in awe.

The large staircase glimmered brightly as it spiralled upwards. A red velvet carpet ran up the centre. As Aziza climbed the stairs, she felt like a princess in her very own fairy tale. Right down to her special dress.

At the top of the stairs, Aziza stopped, suddenly unsure which way led to Peri's room. There were so many doors. *Which one is the right one? I can't remember!*

About the Authors

Lola Morayo is the pen name for the creative partnership of writers Tọ́lá Okogwu and Jasmine Richards.

Tọ́lá is a journalist and author of the Daddy Do My Hair series. She is an avid reader who enjoys spending time with her family and friends in her home in Kent, where she lives with her husband and daughters.

Jasmine is the founder of an inclusive fiction studio called Storymix and has written more than fifteen books for children. She lives in Hertfordshire with her husband and two children.

Both are passionate about telling stories that are inclusive and joyful.

About the Illustrator

Cory Reid lives in Kettering and is an illustrator and designer who has worked in the creative industry for more than fifteen years with clients including, Usborne Publishing, Owlet Press and Card Factory.